I Never Know How Poems Start

Poems by Michael Rosen
Illustrations by Yuliya Somina

Collins

Contents

Introduction

My name's Michael Rosen and
I write poems. I do other things as
well – like talking on the radio – and
I also spend a lot of time visiting
schools and talking to children
about my poems. Sometimes
I suggest that they can write in
ways I do.

I first started writing poems when
I was about 16 and I've been doing it ever since.

Poems come in many different shapes and sizes, they
can sound as if all sorts of different people are speaking
and they can be about very different sorts of things.

They can also be very, very serious, about the most
awful and tragic things, or they can be full of silliness
and nonsense – and all sorts in-between.

I never know how poems start.

Sometimes it's something that I hear.

Sometimes it's something I see.

Sometimes it's something I remember.

Sometimes it's something I imagine.

Sometimes it's something I read.

Sometimes it's some of these things all at the same time.

A thing I've heard could be a sound like
the screech of a sea gull or someone saying,
"I lost my tooth down the toilet."

A thing I've seen could be anything I think looks interesting, like how the back of my hand looks like a map, or an angry man at the bus stop.

A thing I remember comes to me when I daydream, like remembering where I used to play, or what my grandmother's house was like.

A thing I imagine can also be part of a daydream where I say to myself, "What if ...", like, "What if my cat ran away or what if my foot went shopping ..."

A thing I read can be a thought that comes to me as I read, like wondering what people in stories are thinking and remembering.

5

Wrong

We went on holiday with
Mr Wrong.
Everything we said, he said was
Wrong.

He asked us
if night came before day
or day before night.
We said that day came before night.
He said,
Wrong.

So we said night came before day.
He said,
Wrong.

He asked us which came first,
Sunday or Monday.
We said, Sunday.
He said,
Wrong.

So we said,
Monday.
He said,
Wrong.

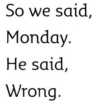

He asked us if he was telling fibs.
We said, yes.
He said,
Wrong.

7

He asked us if he was telling the truth.
We said, yes.
He said,
Wrong.

Then we asked him,
Why are you asking us all these questions?
He said it was because
we liked it.
And we said,
Wrong.

8

This poem started out from something I remember someone saying: when I was a boy we went on holiday with a man who loved asking us questions and telling us we were wrong.

"Wrong!" he kept shouting.

I like poems that have bits in them that are repeated, a "chorus" or "refrain". This means that when I read the poem to other people, they know what's coming and can join in.

Then I like to surprise people by changing something to do with the last chorus. I think surprises in poems are what makes them interesting.

The One You Stop Is You

We met me in a shelter
waiting for a bus.
We said we didn't like me.
I was afraid of us.
We stood in my way,
to stop me getting on the bus,
but the driver would only drive
if I was on the bus.
So we all got on
as I was one of us.

I heard some boys at a bus stop saying they didn't like someone. I thought: they don't realise that the people they say they don't like are actually very like themselves.

So, to show that, I wrote: "We met me in a shelter ..." and "We said we didn't like me ..."

I was trying to say that "me" and "them" are all part of "we".

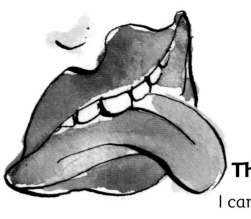

The Five Senses

I can't see my own eyes,
I know because I looked;
I can't hear myself snore,
I tried but I fell asleep;
I can't taste my own tongue
because my tongue gets in the way;
I can't smell my own nose
because I can't turn my nose inside out;
and the tip of my finger can't touch the tip of itself
because the tip of my finger is on the tip of my finger.

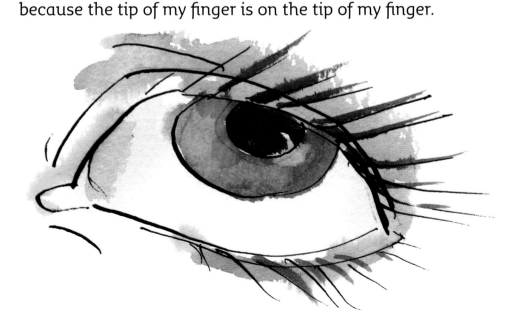

When I write, I like turning really well-known things into things that we don't know. I was thinking about my eyes and isn't it strange that they can't see themselves? Then one evening I started thinking about the other four senses too. Some things are impossible so we have to imagine them. Impossible things are fun to write about!

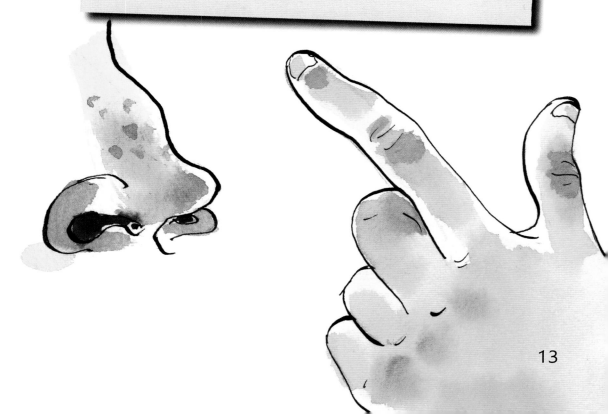

13

Where Broccoli Comes From

Not many people know
that broccoli grows in the armpits
of very big green men
who live in the forest,
and brave broccoli cutters
go deep into the forests
and they creep up on
the very big green men.
They wait for the very
big green men
to fall asleep
and the broccoli cutters get out
their great big broccoli razors
and they shave the armpits
of the very big green men.
And that's where broccoli comes from.
Not many people know that.

Just thought I'd let you know.

I always find it great fun to pretend to be someone else when I write poems. I was thinking here that I could pretend to be an expert on where things come from and how things grow, but really getting it all wrong.

15

True

Nothing rhymes with nothing.
Nobody knows nobody.
Does nothing rhyme with nobody?
Nobody knows nothing.

16

I like making up puzzles. Nothing rhymes with the word "nothing" except for the word "nothing". There isn't anybody in the world who doesn't know anyone at all.

The word "nothing" doesn't rhyme with "nobody" but perhaps there is a word that rhymes with "nobody". There isn't anyone who knows nothing at all.

The House, the Dog and Mr Robinson

In the house
behind the broken fence
where the brambles have smothered the path
and the bricks have fallen out of the wall
lives a dog who growls and winks.

No one goes near the house
behind the broken fence
where the brambles have smothered the path
and the bricks have fallen out of the wall
where there's a dog who growls and winks.

The dog growls and winks
because Mr Robinson tells him jokes
and as Mr Robinson tells the dog jokes
Mr Robinson growls and winks.

Knock knock, says Mr Robinson.
Ruff ruff, says the dog – but he means
"Who's there?"
Cat, says Mr Robinson and he knows that his
dog will be interested in cats.
Ruff ruff, says the dog – but he means, of course,
"Cat who?"
Catch this, says Mr Robinson,
and Mr Robinson throws the dog an old sock
and Mr Robinson growls and winks.

In the house
behind the broken fence
where the brambles have smothered the path
and the bricks have fallen out of the wall
lives a dog who growls and winks.
I'm telling knock knock jokes
the old dog thinks.

There's a house near us that looks just like this. I was with my children on a bus when we saw the house. I started to make up this story about a dog who I imagined lived there. We came home and I started writing it down.

If

Imagine if your nails were nails
so every time they got long
you could hammer them in a bit to make them short.

Imagine if your sink sinks
so every time you had a wash
it would get lower and lower.

Imagine if your painting was painting
so every time you looked at it,
you'd see the painting painting itself.

Imagine if a letter was a letter
then when you opened it
there would be only one letter:
an "a" or an "f" or whatever.

Imagine if the stars were stars
so when you looked up at the sky at night,
it would be full of famous people from the movies.

*I like playing with words.
The longer I look at a word,
the more odd things I seem
to find in it, and all sorts of
different meanings and ideas
pop out.*

Can You See a Noise?

Can you see a noise?
Can you see a picture of noise?
Can you hear a noisy silence?
Or hear a silent noise?
Can you smell a noisy smell?
Or smell a smelly noise?
Can you taste a noisy taste?
Or taste a tasty noise?
Can you feel a noisy noise?
Is there a noise you can feel?
Like a cold noise
a hot noise
a dry noise
a wet noise?
Is that a noisy picture?
Is that the picture of noise?

I Invented the Frisbee

On a camping trip
my brother and me
invented the Frisbee.

Frisbees that spin as they fly
as they zoom, as they dip.
A Frisbee:
it's a disc, a satellite,
a UFO, a spaceship.

The Frisbee –
that looks like it should hum
or whirr or buzz.
It doesn't even whisper.
It flies or spins.
That's what it does.

On a camping trip
my brother and me
invented the Frisbee.
I was seven
My brother was 11.

We were washing the dishes –
thin, lightweight picnic plates.
My brother and me got bored.
It was getting late.

So we started throwing plates
that spin as they fly
as they zoom, as they dip.
Look! That plate is
a disc, a satellite,
a UFO, a spaceship.
A plate
that looks like it should hum
or whirr or buzz.
It doesn't even whisper.
It flies and spins.
That's what it does.

No one knows
my brother and me
invented the Frisbee
on a camping trip
in 1953 ...
... because we didn't
ever tell anyone
we did.

I like playing Frisbee, and every time I do it, it reminds me of when I was a boy, going camping and throwing camping plates. I tried hard to find words to describe Frisbees and camping plates flying through the air. That took me a long time!

How my poems start

My poems start from things I've heard, seen, remembered, imagined or read – and so can yours!

I heard some boys at a bus stop
saying they didn't like someone.
I thought: they don't realise people
like this are actually very like
themselves.
We met me in a shelter
waiting for a bus.
We said we didn't like me.
I was afraid of us.

I was with my children on a bus when
we saw the house. I started to make up
this story about a dog who I imagined
lived there.

In the house
behind the broken fence
where the brambles have smothered the path
and the bricks have fallen out of the wall
lives a dog who growls and winks.

I like playing Frisbee, and every time I do it, it reminds me of when I was a boy. Frisbees that spin as they fly as they zoom, as they dip.

Some things are impossible so we have to imagine them.
I can't smell my own nose because I can't turn my nose inside out.

In one of William Shakespeare's plays someone says, "I see a voice."
Can you hear a noisy silence?
Or hear a silent noise?

Ideas for reading

Written by Clare Dowdall, PhD
Lecturer and Primary Literacy Consultant

Reading objectives:
- listen to, discuss and express views about a wide range of contemporary poetry
- explain and discuss their understanding of poems, both those that they listen to and those that they read for themselves
- discuss their favourite words and phrases

Spoken language objectives:
- use spoken language to develop understanding through speculating, imagining and exploring ideas
- select and use appropriate registers for effective communication
- articulate and justify answers and opinions

Curriculum links: Citizenship; Art and Design

Interest words: silliness, chorus, refrain, broccoli, smothered, Frisbee, satellite, lightweight

Word count: 1,840

Resources: ICT

Build a context for reading

- Explain to the children that they will be reading a book about writing poetry by Michael Rosen. Ask the children if they know any Michael Rosen poems, e.g. "We're Going on a Bear Hunt".

- Look at the front cover and read the title and blurb together. Establish that Michael Rosen is saying he never knows how his poems will start before he begins to write them. Discuss whether children find it easy to write poems.

- Walk through the book together. Help children to notice that each poem is followed by a commentary that is written by Michael Rosen and describes the inspiration for each poem and provides information about his writing.

Understand and apply reading strategies

- Ask children to read the introduction on pp3–5 to find out about Michael Rosen and where his ideas for poems come from. Discuss his list of inspirations and ask children to think of examples of things that they have seen that day at school that could be the starting point for a poem.

- Ask the children to read the poem "Wrong" quietly to themselves, then ask for a volunteer to read it to the group. Discuss whether the children have ever met anyone like this, and how it made them feel.